MOONBEAM
AND THE
ROCKET RIDE

SELMA AND JACK
WASSERMANN

ILLUSTRATIONS
GEORGE ROHRER

BENEFIC PRESS · CHICAGO

Publishing Division of Beckley-Cardy Company

Atlanta   Dallas   Long Beach   Portland

The Moonbeam Books

Copyright 1965 by Benefic Press
All Rights Reserved
Printed in the United States of America

CONTENTS

"Push the Button!"

This is the rocket port.

Men work here.

Rockets go up

from the rocket port.

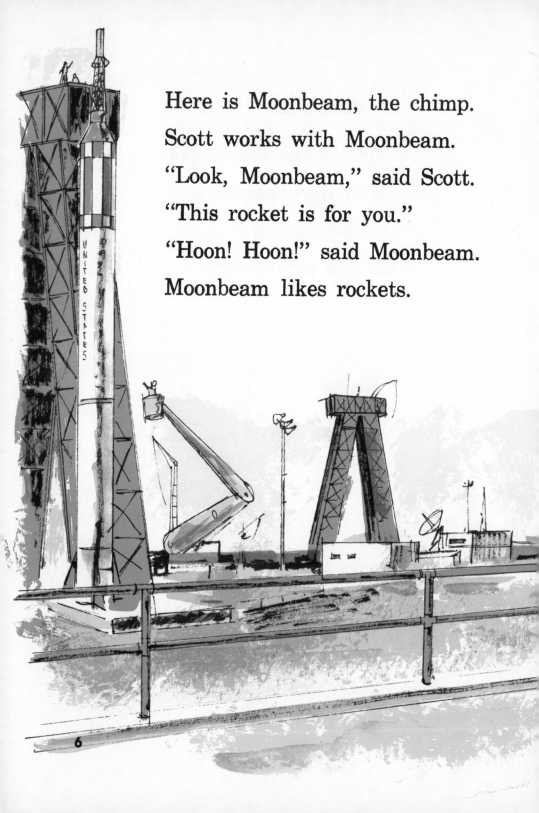

Here is Moonbeam, the chimp.
Scott works with Moonbeam.
"Look, Moonbeam," said Scott.
"This rocket is for you."
"Hoon! Hoon!" said Moonbeam.
Moonbeam likes rockets.

"Tomorrow you will go up
in the rocket," said Scott.

"We will see what the rocket
ride is like for you.

We want to find out
if the rocket is good to ride in."

"Here we are,"
said Scott.
"Come on,
Moonbeam.
We have work
to do."
Moonbeam went in
with Scott.

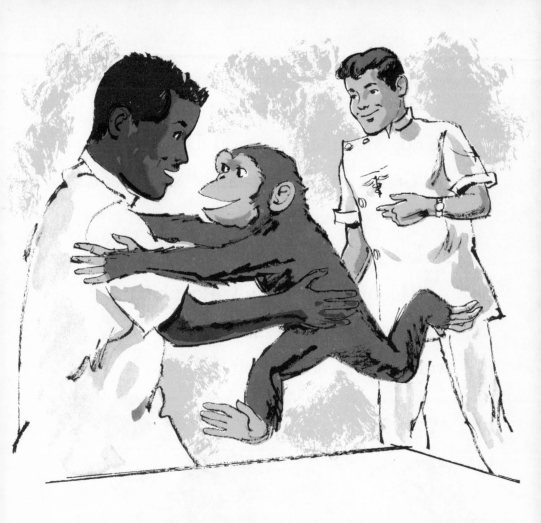

"Look!" said Scott.

"Dr. Jim is here."

Moonbeam ran to Dr. Jim.

Then she jumped up on him.

Dr. Jim laughed.

"Here is the work for you
to do, Moonbeam," said Dr. Jim.

"Come on, Moonbeam," said Scott.

"Do you want to have a good
rocket ride tomorrow?"

"Hoon! Hoon!" said Moonbeam.

"Then you will have to do this
work now," said Scott.

"Push, Moonbeam,"
said Dr. Jim.
"Push the button."

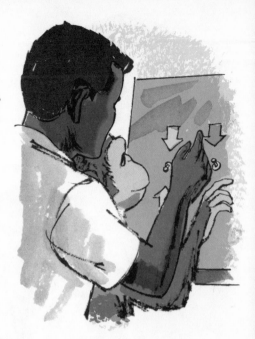

Moonbeam pushed.

"Good!"
said Dr. Jim.
"Now push
the other one."

Moonbeam pushed the other button.

"Good work, Moonbeam!" said Scott.

"Here is something good for you,"
said Dr. Jim.

"It is something you like to eat."

"Hoon! Hoon!" said Moonbeam.

"Now you will
go on a ride,"
said Scott.

"You will have
work to do on the
ride," said Dr. Jim.

"You will have
to push the buttons."

Moonbeam looked
at the ride.

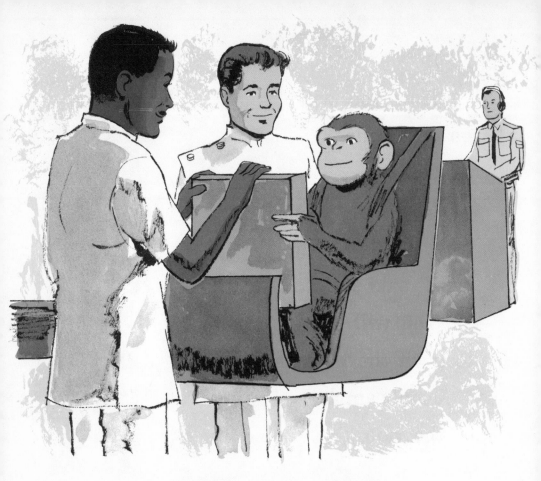

Around and Around

"Jump in!" said Scott.

Moonbeam jumped in.

"Here are the buttons," said Dr. Jim.

Moonbeam looked at the buttons.

Then men pushed some other buttons.

Away went Moonbeam on her ride!
Around and around it went.
Around and around went Moonbeam.
"Heeeeeeeeeeeen!" said Moonbeam.
Faster and faster she went.

"Push the button!" said Dr. Jim.

"Heeeeeeeeeeeeen!" said Moonbeam.

She did not push the button.

"Push it, Moonbeam! Push!" said Scott.

"Heeeeeeeeeeeeen!" said Moonbeam.

Then Moonbeam pushed the button.

"Not too good," said Dr. Jim.

"Will she push her buttons tomorrow in the rocket?". said Scott.

"We will have to see," said Dr. Jim.

"Stop the ride!"
said Dr. Jim.
Little by little
the ride stopped.
But Moonbeam did
not stop.
She jumped out.
And she went
around and around.

On and on
she went.
Around and
away she went.
And then,
out she went!

Scott and Dr. Jim
ran out, too.
"Look out!"
said Scott.

Moonbeam did not see General
Winters and the other men.
They did not see Moonbeam.
Around and around went Moonbeam.

"Moonbeam! Look!"
said Scott.

But Moonbeam
did not see.

She ran into
General Winters.

Down went Moonbeam!

Down went General Winters!

"OOOOFFFF!" said General Winters.

"Heen! Heen!" said Moonbeam.

Scott and Dr. Jim helped the General.

"What is this?" said General Winters.

"Moonbeam was working," said Scott.

"She will go up in a rocket tomorrow," said Dr. Jim.

Then General Winters laughed.

"Do not do this tomorrow," he said.

"You will not have a good ride."

"Heen! Heen!" said Moonbeam.

"Go on now!" said General Winters.

"Tomorrow will be a big day for you."

Then General Winters and the other men went away.

Scott and Moonbeam went away, too.

Up Goes Moonbeam

Scott and Moonbeam
came to a stop.
"Here we are!"
Scott said.

Moonbeam jumped
out with Scott.
Then they
went in.

"Go to sleep, Moonbeam," said Scott.

Moonbeam did not go to sleep.

"What is it, Moonbeam?" said Scott.

Moonbeam looked at Scott.

"Heeeeen," she went.

"You want to sleep here with me?" said Scott.

"Hoon! Hoon!" said Moonbeam.

Then she jumped in.

Then Moonbeam went to sleep.

But Scott did not sleep.

"Now I can not sleep!" he said.

"Hon! Hon!" said Moonbeam

in her sleep.

Day came.

Moonbeam jumped up.

"Hoon! Hoon!" she said.

She wanted to go to the rocket.

"Not too fast, Moonbeam," said Scott.

Scott did not look too good.

"Put this on, Moonbeam,"
said Dr. Jim.

Moonbeam put it on.

Scott and Dr. Jim laughed.

"You look like a push-button chimp,"
said Scott.

28

"Here it is!"
said Scott.
Men worked
on the big rocket.
"Come on now,
Moonbeam," said
Dr. Jim.
"We will help
you into the
big rocket."

Dr. Jim and
Scott went up
with Moonbeam.

Dr. Jim and Scott
helped Moonbeam.
Then the two
men went down.
The other men
stopped working
on the rocket.
They went
away from it.

Dr. Jim and
Scott looked
at the rocket.
The other
men looked, too.
Then a voice
said, "Three...
Two... One...
GO!"
Up went
the big rocket!

A Voice Comes to Moonbeam

Faster, faster, faster, faster
went the rocket.

It went too fast for Moonbeam!

"Heeeeen! Heeeeen!" said Moonbeam.

"Heeeeeeeeeeeeeeen!"

Up and up
went the
big rocket.

Then a big part
of the rocket
came away.

Moonbeam's part
went up and on.

The ride made
Moonbeam want to
jump up and down.

Then a voice came to Moonbeam.

It said, "You can not jump now, Moonbeam.

Be good, Moonbeam."

Moonbeam looked around.

It was the voice of Dr. Jim.

"Now, Moonbeam,"
said Dr. Jim.

"Push the buttons."
But Moonbeam did
not push the buttons.
Moonbeam wanted
to jump around.

"This is not good," said Scott.

"She will do it," said Dr. Jim.

"You have work to do, Moonbeam,"
said Dr. Jim.

"Now push the buttons."

Moonbeam looked at the buttons.

"Push, Moonbeam, push!" came
the voice of Dr. Jim.

Then Moonbeam pushed.

"Good work, Moonbeam!"
said Dr. Jim.

Now Moonbeam liked her rocket ride.

She did not want to jump now.

She looked around and around.

She looked down.

"Hoon! Hoon!" said Moonbeam.

The voice of Dr. Jim came.

"The rocket is not going
where we want it to go," he said.

"We can not see where it will
come down."

Then the voice stopped.

But the rocket went on.

On and on it went.

Up and up it went.

Then down it came!

Down,

 down,

  down

   went the rocket.
Faster and faster
it went.
Faster, faster,
and faster went
Moonbeam, too.
 "Heeeeeeeeeen!
Heeeeeeeeen!" she said.

Down and
down came
the rocket.
Now it did
not go too fast.
But Moonbeam
did not like the
ride down.

CR - R - RUMP!

The rocket came to a stop.

Moonbeam did not want to look.

Then she did look out.

She saw that the rocket was down.

Moonbeam Finds a House

Moonbeam looked
around.

She wanted to be
out of the rocket.

Then she went
to work.

Little by little
she worked her way
up and out.

Moonbeam looked
one way.
She looked the
other way.
It looked like a
good way to go.
Away she went.

On and on
went Moonbeam.
She went and
went and went.
Then Moonbeam
did not go fast.
Now Moonbeam
was lost.

Then Moonbeam came to a stop.

She saw something.

It was not the rocket port.

She did not see one rocket.

It was a house!

Moonbeam ran up to have a look.

Moonbeam looked in.

She looked up and down.

Then she saw something.

It was something that she liked.

Moonbeam wanted to have it.

Moonbeam looked
for a way to go in.
She looked around.
Then she saw a
way to do it.
She worked her
way up.
She jumped in.

Soon Moonbeam was eating.

It was good!

Then a boy came in.

It was Larry Brown.

The boy stopped where he was.

"Mother!" he said.

"Father! Mother! Come fast!"

Mrs. Brown came in.

"What is it, Larry?" she said.

Then she saw Moonbeam.

"A chimp! A little chimp!" she said.

Mr. Brown came, too.

"A chimp? Here?" he said.

A New Friend for Moonbeam

"What will we do with this little chimp?" said Mrs. Brown

"She can be a friend for me," said Larry.

"Where are you from, little chimp?" said Mr. Brown.

But Moonbeam did not look at them. She saw a button.

Moonbeam pushed the button.

"I can not see!" said Larry.

"Ooops!" said Mrs. Brown.

"Ouch!" said Mr. Brown.

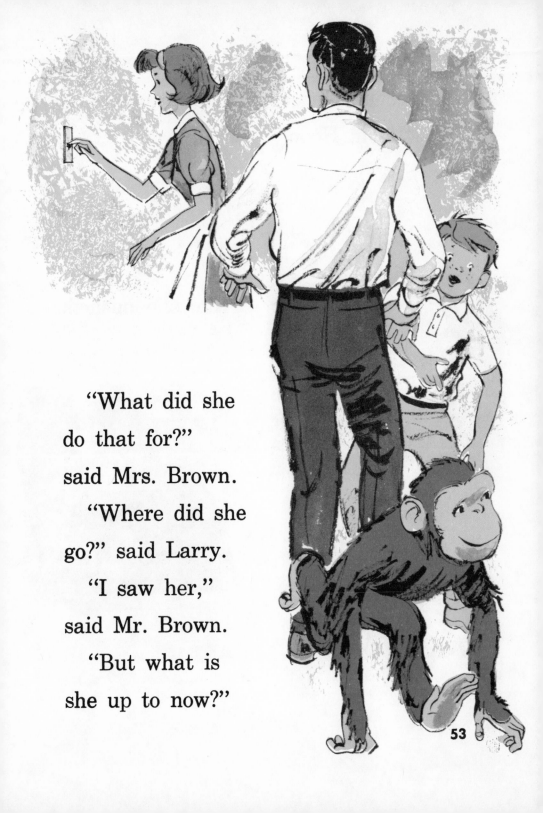

"What did she
do that for?"
said Mrs. Brown.
"Where did she
go?" said Larry.
"I saw her,"
said Mr. Brown.
"But what is
she up to now?"

Moonbeam saw other buttons.
"Hoon! Hoon!" she said.
She pushed.

And she pushed.

And she pushed.

54

And she pushed.

And she pushed.

"Stop, little chimp!" said Larry.

"Look at this house!" said
Mrs. Brown.

Moonbeam looked at her.

"Be a good little chimp now,"
said Mr. Brown.

They came for her.

Moonbeam ran away.

Then Moonbeam stopped.

She saw a picture.

In the picture was Moonbeam!

She saw Scott and Dr. Jim in the picture.

"Hoon! Hoon!" said Moonbeam.

Mr. Brown looked at the picture, too.

"Now I see!" he said.

"This is the chimp from the rocket port!"

"She was on a rocket ride
and was lost," said Mr. Brown.

"We will help her go back to the
rocket port."

"Will she have to go?" Larry said.

"She will have to," said his father.

Larry looked down.

He did not like it.

Soon Scott and Dr. Jim came.

When Moonbeam saw Scott, she ran up to him fast.

Then she jumped on him.

"It is good to see you, Moonbeam," said Scott.

"Hoon! Hoon!" said Moonbeam.

Mrs. Brown and Mr. Brown laughed at Moonbeam.

But Larry did not laugh.

He looked down.

Dr. Jim saw him.

"What is it?" he said.

"I wanted Moonbeam for a friend,"
said Larry.

"I do not want her to go away!"

"You and Moonbeam can be friends,"
said Dr. Jim.

"You can come to see her at the
rocket port."

"I can?" said Larry.

"Scott and I will see to it,"
said Dr. Jim.

"I will come," Larry said.

"Come, Moonbeam," said Scott.

"We will have to go now."

"See you soon, Moonbeam," said Larry.

"Hoon! Hoon!"
said Moonbeam.

Then she went
away with Scott
and Dr. Jim.

VOCABULARY

The total number of different words in this book, excluding proper names, is 102. Seven of these words are first grade level and are listed below in roman type. Seven words are above first grade level and are shown below in italic type. The number after the word indicates the page on which it first appears.

button 5	other 11
chimp 6	*part* 33
	port 5
faster 15	*push* 5
friend 51	
if 7	*rocket* 5
lost 45	tomorrow 7
men 30	voice 32